# BOBOS BABES

## ADVENTURES

# A Magical Halloween

Written by    Karen M. Bobos

Illustrated by    Jazinel Libranda

Please visit BobosBabes.com

Published by Bobos Babes, Ltd.

ISBN: 978-1-7374375-6-7 Hardback Edition

ISBN: 978-1-7374375-7-4 Paperback Edition

United States

# Dedication

To my husband, Stephen -- my love, my heart, my forever --
He carries my spirit through every crazy endeavor.
We met at a wedding on Halloween in two thousand nine.
Instantly, I was forever his and he was forever mine.
Halloween is a holiday that our family will always hold dear.
We celebrate with a family-themed costume year after year.

The wind whistled through the window
That was opened just a crack
While the curtains blew with a rhythm,
Forward and back.

Fairy Cora wrapped her shawl around her shoulders
As she cozied in her chair,
Glancing out the window
At the colorful leaves that fell through the air.

Angel Scarlett poured her sisters
Another cup of hot apple cider.
Princess Daphne tucked her feet
Into her throw blanket a little tighter.

"I just love the fall season
And baking warm treats," Angel Scarlett said.
"Would anyone like a piece
Of my homemade pumpkin-apple bread?"

"Oh, I would just love a piece," said Princess Daphne.
"I was just about to ask.
And after we eat, let's go shopping,
So we can each pick out a Halloween mask."

"Earlier, Gavin the Grasshopper
From Lily the Ladybug's Boutique gave us a call,"
Said Fairy Cora. "He invited us to see this year's masks
Displayed on their wall."

Lily the Ladybug's
BOUTIQUE

That afternoon, the magical sisters
Hopped on their giant dog, Luke, for a ride
Across the land of Harmony to the boutique;
The owner greeted them outside.

"Hello, Bobos Babes," said Lily the Ladybug to the sisters,
"So happy you're here!
Come inside. Let's find a mask that you will love
… and other people may fear."

Lily the Ladybug made a scary face,
which caused Cora and Scarlett to laugh.
Princess Daphne got scared and screamed,
and her sisters said, "Oh Daph!"

"Actually, my brother, Gavin,
has put three special, custom-made masks aside."
Lily put her hand to her mouth and whispered,
"Shhhh … They're classified."

"What do you mean?" said Fairy Cora.
"What makes them so unique?"
"Well, come inside, Bobos Babes," Lily said.
"You'll have to take a peek."

Luke held his paw over his eyes
As Lily the Ladybug held the shop door open wide.
Fairy Cora and Angel Scarlett were filled with excitement
As they went inside.

Princess Daphne was a little hesitant,
But her sense of adventure kicked in.
"I'm not afraid of a silly mask!" she said,
Entering the shop with a confident grin.

In the back corner of the boutique
Was a door and under it was a glowing light.
Lily led the sisters toward it,
And as they got closer, the light became bright.

When they opened the door,
They saw Gavin the Grasshopper was in the room.
The mysterious light that they saw was coming
From his lightning bug costume.

"Oh hello, Bobos Babes!" said Gavin,
Who worked at the shop for his sister, Lily.
"I was just trying on my Halloween costume.
Do you like it, or do I look silly?"

"Oh, it's great!" said Fairy Cora.
"I just love how it lights up and looks so real."
"Thanks!" Gavin said. "I used my employee discount
And got it for a steal."

"Come, ladies, we placed your special masks
Over here," Lily the Ladybug said,
Pointing to three boxes, each tied
With a velvet ribbon in her signature color, red.

Each sister took a box, but as they were
About to open them up, Lily said,
"You must wait until Halloween day
Before putting your mask on your head."

"But Halloween is tomorrow," said Princess Daphne.
"What if mine doesn't fit?"
Gavin said, "It will. We used last year's measurement
When custom-creating it."

"Why do we have to wait until Halloween
To try them on?" asked Angel Scarlett.
Lily said, "Actually, you need to wait
Until noon tomorrow. Please don't forget."

Fairy Cora was confused. "Well, that doesn't make sense.
What's the big deal?
Were you able to make me a witch mask?" she said.
"Did you make it look real?"

"These masks are our best work ever!"
Gavin reassured. "That is all we can say.
If you'd rather, you can pick a mask from the wall
Where the rest are on display."

"We can be patient and wait until tomorrow
To open our masks," said Daphne.
Lily said, "Trust us. You will have the best costumes
In all of the land of Harmony."

Scarlett said, "Yes, we can wait
To open our masks until tomorrow at noon."
Gavin said, "It is crucial that you
Do not open them even a minute too soon."

The sisters agreed to the rules
And bought the special masks for Halloween,
But that night felt like the longest night
That the Bobos Babes had ever seen.

Halloween finally arrived,
And the Bobos Babes were filled with anticipation.
"I cannot wait any longer!"
Cried Fairy Cora, reaching a point of desperation.

Fairy Cora used her power of swiftness
To fly quickly toward her wrapped box.
"No! It's not noon yet!" yelled Angel Scarlett,
Who was staring at three clocks.

Just then, their grandfather clock struck noon,
And the sisters jumped with glee.
They each grabbed their box
And unwrapped their masks as carefully as could be.

Each sister looked inside her box at her mask
And couldn't believe her eyes.
"Mine is clear. It looks like glass,"
Said Princess Daphne with a look of surprise.

"Mine too," said Angel Scarlett.
"I can see right through it. It's transparent."
Inside was a card that read,
"It's what's real that matters, not the apparent."

Scarlett tried the mask on her face
And began to laugh. She said, "Oh, it tickles."
Just then, she transformed into a
Blue monster covered with hot pink dimples.

"Ahhhh!" screamed Cora and Daphne
As they scurried to hide under a bed.
"What's the matter?" said Scarlett,
Touching the mask she just put on her head.

"You're a monster!" said Cora,
Holding onto Daphne and trembling with fear.
"Really? That's awesome!" said Angel Scarlett
As she ran to look into the mirror.

"Oh my goodness!" said Angel Scarlett.
"You cannot even tell that it's me.
I was hoping Lily would make me
A monster mask that looked super scary."

Fairy Cora crawled out from under the bed
And ran to try on her mask as well.
She read its card out loud,
"You have six hours from noon to enjoy the spell."

Cora put on her clear mask
And all of a sudden there was a boom and a switch.
Daphne, still under the bed, screamed,
As Fairy Cora turned into a green witch.

"Am I a witch?" Cora saw her green hands
And then ran to the mirror to look.
Fairy Cora and Angel Scarlett were amazed
At the transformation they took.

"Come on, Princess Daphne! Put on your mask,"
Said Scarlett. "It's your turn."
Daphne slowly came out from under the bed
With a look of worry and concern.

She opened her box and saw that it had a card
Enclosed with an important task.
She read it, "At 6 o'clock, be in the exact room
Where you put on your mask."

Daphne put on her mask, and a cloud of
Smoke encircled her. When it cleared
Fairy Cora and Angel Scarlett saw
That their middle sister had disappeared.

"Daphne!" The sisters' hearts dropped
As they wondered where their sister was.
"Boo!" blurted Princess Daphne.
Scarlett and Cora screamed and then paused.

"Daphne?" questioned Fairy Cora
As she heard a giggle from the air.
"I'm a ghost!" Princess Daphne said,
Her voice seeming to come from nowhere.

"These masks are AWESOME!"
Exclaimed Princess Daphne, still unseen.
"Let's go Trick-or-Treating.
This is going to be the best-ever Halloween!"

The Bobos Babes had a blast,
Trick-or-Treating around the town.
No one knew who they were.
Their identity was safe and sound.

Neither Leonard the Lion, the Bobcat Family
nor the Swans knew who they were.
Cora said, "Our friends had no clue
That we were the ghost, witch, and monster!"

At six o'clock, the sisters were in their castle
As instructed, in their bedroom.
Their costumes vanished,
And their Angel, Princess, and Fairy identities resumed.

"OMG!" said Angel Scarlett.
"Those were the best Halloween costumes ever!
Lily the Ladybug and Gavin the Grasshopper
Are so talented and clever."

The Bobos Babes stared in the mirror,
Amazed that the costumes were gone.
Suddenly, Daphne was missing,
And her sisters worried something went wrong.

"Where's Daphne?" said Angel Scarlett,
Wondering if the spell wasn't broke.
"Boo!" shouted Daphne,
Popping out from behind the mirror, playing a joke.

"Daphne!" the sisters jumped, startled,
And then the three girls began to laugh.
When they caught their breath from laughing,
Scarlett and Cora said, "Oh Daph!"

The sisters giggled all night,
Reminiscing how the day felt like a wild dream,
And they all agreed that this year was by far
Their most magical Halloween!

Made in the USA
Middletown, DE
18 October 2021